Dear Parent:
Your child's love of reading starts here!

Every child learns to read in a different way and at his or her own speed. Some go back and forth between reading levels and read favorite books again and again. Others read through each level in order. You can help your young reader improve and become more confident by encouraging his or her own interests and abilities. From books your child reads with you to the first books he or she reads alone, there are I Can Read Books for every stage of reading:

SHARED READING
Basic language, word repetition, and whimsical illustrations, ideal for sharing with your emergent reader

BEGINNING READING
Short sentences, familiar words, and simple concepts for children eager to read on their own

READING WITH HELP
Engaging stories, longer sentences, and language play for developing readers

READING ALONE
Complex plots, challenging vocabulary, and high-interest topics for the independent reader

ADVANCED READING
Short paragraphs, chapters, and exciting themes for the perfect bridge to chapter books

I Can Read Books have introduced children to the joy of reading since 1957. Featuring award-winning authors and illustrators and a fabulous cast of beloved characters, I Can Read Books set the standard for beginning readers.

A lifetime of discovery begins with the magical words **"I Can Read!"**

Visit www.icanread.com for information
on enriching your child's reading experience.

For my father
—A.S.C.

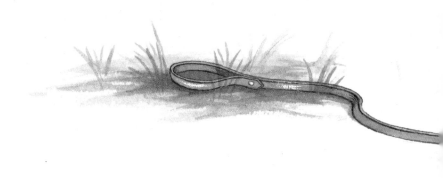

12 13 14 15/0 • Printed in the U.S.A.
40 • First Scholastic printing, March 2010

I Can Read!™

SHARED
My
First
READING

Biscuit Takes a Walk

story by ALYSSA SATIN CAPUCILLI
pictures by PAT SCHORIES

SCHOLASTIC INC.
New York Toronto London Auckland
Sydney Mexico City New Delhi Hong Kong

Time for a walk, Biscuit.

Woof, woof!

3

It's time for a walk
to Grandpa's house.

Let's go!

Woof, woof!

Time for a walk, Biscuit.

Woof, woof!

Biscuit wants to dig.

Time for a walk, Biscuit.

Woof, woof!

Biscuit wants to roll.

Funny puppy!
It's time for a walk
to Grandpa's house.

Let's go!

Woof, woof!

Time for a walk, Biscuit.

Woof, woof!

Biscuit wants to see

the squirrels.

Time for a walk, Biscuit.

Woof, woof!

Biscuit wants
to see the birds.

Silly puppy!
It's time for a walk
to Grandpa's house.
Woof!

15

Wait, Biscuit. Come back.

Grandpa's house is this way!

Woof, woof!

Oh, Biscuit!

What do you see now?

Woof, woof!

It's Grandpa!

Woof, woof!

A walk to Grandpa's house
is fun, Biscuit.

But a walk with Grandpa

is the best walk of all.

Time for a walk, Biscuit.

A walk for everyone.

Woof, woof!